Sparky's
Bad Spell

www.rand

MRS MOTHWICK'S
MAGIC ACADEMY

OUT-
BUILDINGS

MOTHWICK
FAMILY'S
CHAMBER

COURTYARD
FOR TRAINING

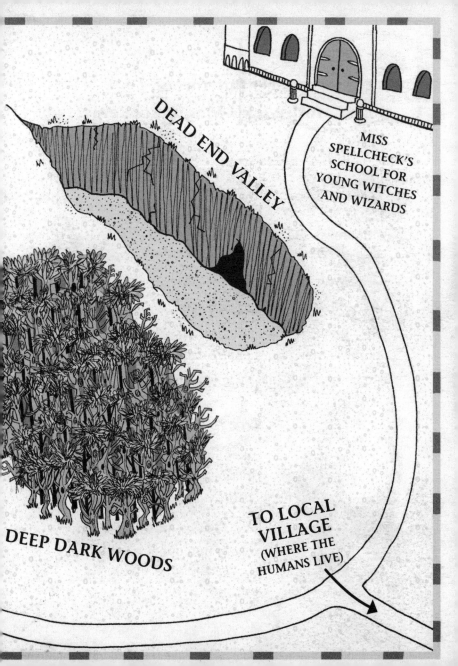

Meet the stars of
Mrs Mothwick's Magic Academy!

Sparky

Sparky is a fluffy, bouncy puppy
with brown and white splodges.
He is adventurous, playful and
very brave, and loves his wizard, Carl.
Mrs Mothwick's Magic Academy has
never allowed puppies in before, but
Sparky is trying hard to prove that he
can learn magic and be a good dog.

Sox

Sox is Sparky's best friend.
She is a sensible kitten with jet-
black fur and white paws. She
loves Sparky and does her best
to keep him out of mischief.

Trixie

Trixie is a sleek black cat. She's very good at magic but is a bit of a bully. She doesn't like dogs, so Sparky had better watch out!

Mrs Mothwick

Mrs Mothwick is head of the Magic Academy. She has a thin, warty face and wears a tall black hat. Her familiar – her special animal friend with whom she has a magical bond – is a gruff vulture called Mr Carrion. She is proud of her Magic Academy, but she worries that her son, Carl, isn't ready to be a wizard.

Carl Mothwick

Carl is a bit clumsy and
scruffy. His shoelaces
always seem to be
untied, and he smells of
mud and chewing gum.
Even though he tries
really hard, poor Carl
just isn't very good at
magic. He never knows

where his wand is, and even when he does
find it, he can't make it work the way the other
trainees can. Carl is desperate to prove to everyone,
including his mum, that he is a proper wizard like
his dad.

Mrs Cackleback

Mrs Cackleback is the only witch ever to
own a terrifying griffin as her familiar,
but the less said about her and her
wicked ways, the better . . .

Sparky's Bad Spell

RUBY NASH

Illustrated by Clare Elsom

RED FOX

SPARKY'S BAD SPELL
A RED FOX BOOK 978 1 782 95299 2

First published in Great Britain by Red Fox,
an imprint of Random House Children's Publishers UK
A Penguin Random House Company

Penguin
Random House
UK

This edition published 2015

1 3 5 7 9 10 8 6 4 2

Series created by Working Partners Limited
Copyright © Working Partners Limited, 2015
Cover and interior illustrations copyright © Clare Elsom, 2015
With special thanks to Pip Jones

Penguin Random House is committed to a sustainable future for
our business, our readers and our planet. This book is made from
Forest Stewardship Council® certified paper.

MIX
Paper from
responsible sources
FSC
www.fsc.org   FSC® C016897

Set in ITC Stone Informal

Red Fox Books are published by Random House Children's Publishers UK,
61–63 Uxbridge Road, London W5 5SA

www.randomhousechildrens.co.uk
www.totallyrandombooks.co.uk
www.randomhouse.co.uk

Addresses for companies within The Random House Group Limited can be
found at: www.randomhouse.co.uk/offices.htm

THE RANDOM HOUSE GROUP Limited Reg. No. 954009

A CIP catalogue record for this book is available from the British Library.

Printed and bound in Great Britain by
CPI Group (UK) Ltd, Croydon CR0 4YY

For Coco and Ruby, who are about
as magic as two people can get

MRS MOTHWICK'S MAGIC ACADEMY

1

Sparky stood beside his wizard, Carl, trying to keep still. He hadn't been at Mrs Mothwick's Magic Academy for long, but he'd already seen most of the training rooms and this one was his favourite. The wallpaper

was dark crimson with a swirly gold pattern, and the windows stretched from the floor to the ceiling. Each one was draped with heavy, red velvet curtains. They smelled old.

"Settle down now, please," said the teacher, Mr Noble, peering over his rectangular glasses.

All around Sparky, the familiars fidgeted nervously next to their owners – apart from an upside-down bat, who swung from his witch's fingertip.

Over the squawks and squeaks
of the birds and animals, Mr Noble
tried again: "Welcome to Beginners'
Magic Class." He puffed out his
plump, rosy cheeks. "It's now time
for you all to demonstrate your
tricks."

Sparky's tail wagged. He pawed
Carl's shoe, and the boy glanced
down and gave him a wink.

"Have you done your homework,
Sox?" Sparky whispered to his best

4

friend, who was sitting next to him.

Sox was a black kitten with white paws that looked like socks. "Yes, we have a trick," she replied, with one ear flattening a little. "But I'm not sure we've practised enough . . ."

Sox's witch, Sophie, bent down and her long hair flopped forward and tickled Sparky's nose.

"What's Sparky saying to you?" Sophie whispered to Sox.

"He wondered," Sox replied,

"whether we'd done our homework and—"

"Sshhh!" came a hiss from behind them.

Sparky turned to see Trixie glaring at them. Her witch, Amelia, flicked her perfect black ponytail snootily. Trixie's perfect black tail swished in time.

They turned to look at Mr Noble as he started speaking.

"The purpose of the homework,"

he said thoughtfully, "was to see
how you familiars and witches
and wizards work together. As we
all know: **A witch is not a
witch without a familiar,
and a familiar is not
a familiar without a
witch**."

Every witch and wizard needed a
familiar – an animal to help them
do magic. Sparky was so happy
that he was Carl's familiar . . . even

though he wasn't much help when it came to magic! But he and Carl had been practising their trick all week. They definitely wouldn't be bottom of the class this time.

"By now," Mr Noble continued, "I expect most of you are managing to communicate with each other with a few words."

Sparky's ears drooped. He still hadn't managed to say a single word that Carl could understand.

"Joshua and Finley," Mr Noble said to a wizard and his ferret familiar. "Why don't you go first with your trick?"

Finley stood on his back legs, looked at Joshua, and squeaked. "*Dook-dook-dook!*"

Joshua shrugged, a worried expression

on his face. He couldn't understand
what his familiar was saying.

Some of the witches giggled.

The ferret frowned in
concentration and tried again.
"*Dook . . . din . . . s-s-spin!*" he finally
squeaked.

Joshua flicked his wand towards
his shoes, creating a cloud of glitter.
Finley began running in a circle
around his feet. The boy stood on
his tiptoes. All the students leaned

forward to watch as Joshua began to spin. He went faster and faster, until he and Finley were just a blur.

"*S-s-s-stop!*" squeaked Finley.

"Yes! Please stop!" Joshua shouted. Finley stopped running, and Joshua, looking very dizzy, slowly came to a halt. Everyone clapped as they staggered back to their places.

"Very good," Mr Noble said. "A slow start, Finley, but you got there

in the end with your words. Well done." He looked around the room. "Now let's see Trixie and Amelia."

"Finally," Trixie muttered as they pushed past Sparky.

When everyone was quiet, Trixie purred: "Allow me to introduce Amelia, the great-great-granddaughter of Madame Marvella, inventor of a thousand potions."

Sparky's heart did an extra beat

when he saw how expert Trixie had become at talking to her witch.

Amelia smiled. "Thank you. And allow me to introduce Trixie, one of seventeen generations of feline familiars."

"They're so good at communicating," Sparky whispered.

"They're so good at being show-offs!" Sox replied.

Amelia flicked her wand and a golden orb of light floated into

the air. Trixie twitched her shiny whiskers. A glittery spark appeared and shot towards the orb.

There was a **flash!**

Then,

Pop!

Bang!

Whizz!

Bright green and gold fireworks began exploding above the heads of all the trainees and familiars. Three white mice, Harry, Larry and Sid, squealed and jumped into their wizards' pockets to hide.

"Thank you, Trixie and Amelia," Mr Noble yelled above the noise. "That's enough now."

Everyone clapped as Trixie and Amelia made their way back to their places, beaming smugly.

"Ah, er . . . Sparky and Carl!"
Mr Noble called.

Sparky's tummy flipped. *This
is it!*

At the front of the class, Carl
took out his slightly bent wand.
"Ready?" he asked Sparky.

The pup shuffled on his paws
and wagged his tail. "Yip!" he
replied. *I'm ready!*

"My wonderful puppy Sparky
and I would like to show you our

amazing tricks," Carl said in a booming voice.

All the trainees grew silent.

Carl held his wand above Sparky's head. "Sit!" he said.

Sparky immediately sat on his bottom. He wagged his tail.

"Play dead!" Carl said.

Sparky rolled onto his back and let his tongue flop out of the side of his mouth. He heard someone sniggering.

Carl fumbled in his pocket and brought out a red rubber ball. Sparky sat up straight and waited.

"Fetch!" Carl yelled as he threw the ball across the room.

Sparky was off like a dart. He caught the ball in his mouth

mid-bounce, then scrambled
back across the wooden floor and
dropped it at Carl's feet.

Carl grinned, scooped up the
ball, then turned to everyone
watching. ***"Ta-da!"***

The whole room went silent for

a moment. Then everyone erupted into laughter. Sparky's tail drooped between his legs.

"Quiet!" Mr Noble shouted. His face was usually kind, but now it looked very stern. "Everyone be quiet."

The class settled down again.

"Carl," Mr Noble said softly. "I can see that you and Sparky have a very strong bond."

Carl's cheeks were bright red

now. He stared at the floor.

"It's just . . ." Mr Noble paused.
"We really need to start seeing you
do some . . . magic."

Carl sighed.

Sparky whined.

Mrs Mothwick's Magic Academy
had never allowed a puppy in
before. Everyone seemed to think
puppies didn't make good familiars.
But Sparky really thought they'd
done well this time. Now it seemed

that poor Carl was going to get the lowest mark – *again*.

All because Sparky wasn't magical.

2

It was just after lunch time and Sparky and the rest of the class were outside in the thick wood beyond the school. A soft breeze billowed and the seeds from a nearby dandelion clock floated silently away.

"I believe you all know about the dangers of the **Deep Dark Wood**?" Mrs Mothwick said to them.

Some of the trainees muttered that they did, while Mrs Mothwick's icy blue eyes rested on her son Carl and Sparky.

"You must be very careful while we are out here. Stay near me and watch out for **grabby trees** and **gulp pits**," Mrs Mothwick added.

Sparky shivered. Grabby trees and gulp pits were the least of their worries. The last time he and Carl were in the **Deep Dark Wood** they were nearly caught by a griffin. Sparky could still remember the scent of the terrifying beast now – half lion, half eagle, a smell so strong it had made his nose hurt.

"**Yip! Arf-rrr!**" Sparky said cheerily to Carl. *At least it's daylight this time!*

Sparky knew Carl couldn't understand what he was saying, so he licked the boy twice on his hand. Carl's face broke into a smile. "We'll be OK, boy."

Sparky panted happily. *We might not be able to speak to each other in words,* he thought, *but we communicate in our own way.*

Sparky looked around at the green, rocky landscape. A little way down the slope was a stream, and to either side were towering cliffs. Funny-looking plants grew out of them at strange angles.

"Many magical plants grow in the wood. And most are to be

found here, in Dead End Valley,"
Mrs Mothwick told the group.
"Gathering magical ingredients is
a very important task, and requires
good teamwork. Witches and
wizards must work together with
their familiars. Your task today is
to find a Shift Root. It's used for the
powerful Shift Shape Spell, which
can make people and animals
change their appearance. It grows
underground and smells like

modelling clay. It can be discovered by using the Sniffy Spell, which you should all know." She raised her hand. "You may begin."

The trainees and familiars scurried off in their pairs. Sparky could hear the young witches and wizards muttering the spell as they flicked their wands:

"Nazba-lee! Nazba-lay! Magic be lent!

Sniffy Spell cast, you will find any scent!"

Sparky looked at Carl, who was scratching his head with one hand and holding his bent wand with the other. "*Naz-aboo! Naz-abay . . . !* No, that's not right," Carl said. "*Naz-ra-boo*? No. Oh, what is it?"

Sparky gave a "Yip!" If only he could tell Carl what the words were.

Just then, a **musty, earthy pong...**

wafted past his nose.

Modelling clay! Sparky didn't
need the spell – he was already
great at sniffing things out. He
yipped and ran off towards a steep
upward slope.

31

"Wait!" Carl shouted, running after him.

But Sparky was too busy snuffling the scent, his nose to the ground.

They followed the stream until a waft of modelling clay made Sparky's head flick sharply left.

"Yip, yip!" Sparky said. *This way!*

Sparky kept sniffing as they approached a wide, spooky-looking cave in the cliff face. The smell of

modelling clay was getting stronger.

"I'm not sure . . ." Carl said,
looking warily into the blackness,
but Sparky really wanted them to
do well. He trotted in.

Sparky waited for his eyes to
adjust to the dark, then stepped
forwards slowly. The smell of
modelling clay was very strong
now. Sparky's nose led him to a
dimly lit corner. On the ground was
a long wooden spoon. Sparky gave

the spoon a good sniff, then picked
it up with his teeth and carried it
over to where Carl was waiting at
the cave entrance.

"You found it, Sparky!" Carl
cried. "Good dog!" Then he looked
at the spoon and laughed. "This
isn't a Shift Root!"

Sparky gave a grumbly growl.
But it smells like one!

Carl walked back out into the
bright sunlight and turned the

spoon in his hands. "It's a cauldron spoon," he said. "Like the ones we use in the Magic Lab. Except . . ."

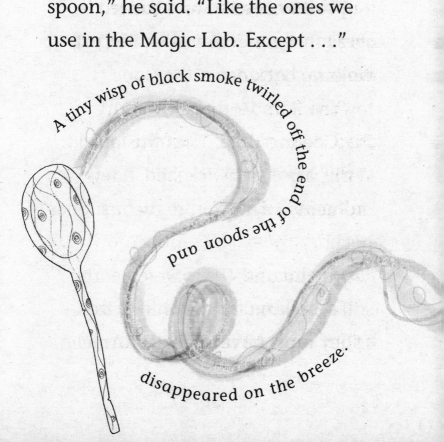

A tiny wisp of black smoke twirled off the end of the spoon and disappeared on the breeze.

Sparky yipped in surprise.

"**Wowzers** – we'd better show this to my mum!" said Carl, walking back down the slope towards Mrs Mothwick.

"Goodness me. That was quick, Carl!" Mrs Mothwick said, a few moments later. "You're the first ones back!"

Amelia and Trixie were nearby, still searching for the Shift Root. "They must have cheated," Amelia

grumbled, glaring at Sparky.

Mr Carrion frowned. "They didn't use magic," he said gruffly. "It's not how we do things."

"Actually, we didn't find the Shift Root," said Carl. "But Sparky found this."

Mrs Mothwick took the spoon, and gasped as another wisp of smoke twirled off it and floated away.

Mr Carrion

squawked in shock.

"Good work, Carl.
Well sniffed, Sparky. Witches!
Familiars!" Mrs Mothwick bellowed
suddenly. "Class is finished!"

"What?" Trixie hissed. "But we
still haven't found the Shift Root—"

Mrs Mothwick ignored Trixie.
"Follow Mr Carrion," she ordered.

The vulture opened one black
wing and beckoned the class towards
him.

Mrs Mothwick quickly stashed the
cauldron spoon inside the folds of
her cloak and scurried away, a deep
frown on her face.

Sparky couldn't work out what was
so upsetting about a wooden spoon.
Even though Mrs Mothwick had said
"Good work," he couldn't help feeling
like he'd messed up again.

MRS MOTHWICK'S MAGIC ACADEMY

3

Mrs Mothwick had asked Carl
and Sparky to come and see her
later that afternoon. The corridor
leading to her office was long and
narrow. Oil paintings of animals
hung on the walls, with name

plaques underneath. Sparky could see cats, rats, bats and squirrels – but not a single puppy. His tummy flipped at the thought of all the magic creatures that had been at the school before him. He didn't feel like he would ever be magical enough to fit in.

Carl was about to knock on Mrs Mothwick's door when Sparky's ears pricked. He could hear her speaking. Carl leaned in.

"It reeks of wicked ways," came Mrs Mothwick's muffled voice.

Sparky heard something wooden clatter on Mrs Mothwick's desk. "I think she's talking about the cauldron spoon,"

he said, but of course Carl couldn't understand him.

Carl whispered, "I think she's talking about the cauldron spoon."

Behind the door, Mr Carrion spoke. "And then there was the griffin in the **Deep Dark Wood**."

"Mrs Cackleback is the only witch who's ever been wicked enough to keep such a fierce familiar," said Mrs Mothwick.

"She's close by – I'm sure of it."

Sparky gasped and looked at
Carl. They had never met Mrs
Cackleback, but she had a fearsome
reputation for wicked ways.

Carl took a deep breath, pursed
his lips and knocked.

"Enter!" Mrs Mothwick called.

Inside, Mrs Mothwick had
removed her hat and was sitting
in a high-backed wooden chair,
frowning. Mr Carrion perched on

the corner of the desk, hunching
so that his bald head just peeped
above his folded black wings.

"Sit down," Mrs Mothwick said.

Sparky sat straight down on his
bottom, like a good dog. Carl sat on
a leather stool.

Mrs Mothwick peered down her
nose. "We need to talk about your
marks, Carl. And about Sparky."

Sparky's tail wagged nervously.
He hoped Mrs Mothwick was going

to say how well they'd done in
finding the strange spoon.

"I'm afraid that you and
Sparky just aren't making enough
progress." She was frowning
but she didn't look cross – more
disappointed, which felt worse.
"Although you did very well in
Dead End Valley today, you're both
failing every class. Spells, potions,
broomstick-flying, familiar history
– and as for communicating, well,

Sparky is getting nowhere."

Sparky's heart sank. He wasn't born with magic like the rest of the animals and students here. He was trying his best, but clearly it wasn't enough.

"Mum, he's working really, really hard," Carl said quietly. "We both are."

"On Monday, members of the GRAND COUNCIL OF WIZARDRY AND WITCHINESS are coming to inspect

the school," said Mrs Mothwick. "I've given Sparky a chance but, as you know, most witches believe that if animals aren't born with magic, they will never be able to learn it."

Carl sighed.

Sparky whined.

Mrs Mothwick continued. "I'm afraid if they discover that we are training an un-magic puppy they might close down the school."

Oh no! Sparky thought. That

would mean he would be sent back to the rescue centre, away from Sox and Carl.

Carl looked pleadingly at his mum. "We'll work even harder," he promised.

Sparky gave a loud **"Yip!"** in agreement.

Mrs Mothwick sighed and gave a small nod, while Mr Carrion grumbled something Sparky didn't quite catch.

I might not be magical, Sparky thought, *but I'll think of something to keep the school open.*

MRS MOTHWICK'S MAGIC ACADEMY

4

Sparky blinked at the bright
morning light streaming through
the stained-glass windows of
the Great Hall. He always felt
a bit nervous in Mr Carrion's
Communication Class.

"In time, all familiars should be able to talk to their trainees perfectly," Mr Carrion said, swooping down to the floor. "Familiars who work very hard may one day be able to speak to all witches and wizards, as I do."

Sparky felt sad. He was so far behind.

"To see how you're coming along, we're going to play a game called 'fetch'," Mr Carrion said,

pacing before the class.

Sparky's head popped up. He was really good at fetch! He tried to stop his tail from wagging, but it kept beating the floor noisily.

"In this task, it will be witches and wizards doing the fetching," Mr Carrion said flatly, staring at Sparky. "Not the familiars."

Oh! Sparky thought. That made things different.

"Amelia, hand those around,"

Mr Carrion ordered, nodding towards a large wicker basket. Amelia pulled out a round glass object. It was the size of a Christmas bauble and it sparkled in the light.

A crystal ball! thought Sparky.

Amelia handed the crystal balls to the boys and girls.

"Hold them above your heads," Mr Carrion said.

The trainees did as they were told. Mr Carrion stuck his hooked

beak under his wing and pulled out
a wand. He flapped into the air,
flew one circuit of the Great Hall,
then swooped down and tapped
each crystal ball with his wand.

"Wowzers!" Carl said, gazing at their ball. "Look, Sparky, it's us!"

Carl held the ball down low so Sparky could take a closer look. Inside the glass was a picture of both their faces.

Sparky wagged his tail.

Mr Carrion landed at the front of the Hall and tucked his wand back under his wing.

"The game is simple," he said.
"Familiars hide the ball somewhere
in the school, then return to their
witch or wizard and explain where
to find it."

Sparky's heart was beating
fast. *How am I going to do this?*
He still hadn't learned how to
communicate magically with Carl.

All the trainees covered their
eyes. "Off you go!" said Mr Carrion.

Next to Sparky, a squirrel picked

up her crystal ball with her front paws, then tottered on her back legs towards the door. In a few moments, all the other animals had left the Great Hall to find a hiding place.

I need to make this really simple, Sparky told himself. He picked up the ball in his mouth and placed it inside Carl's backpack, right next to him.

A few familiars were arriving

back already, telling their trainees where to look. Trixie purred loudly: "Our crystal ball is in the Library, Amelia. Filed under 'C', next to *Freezing Spells* by Dr Cryogen." Amelia strutted off to find it.

Sparky tapped Carl's shoe with his paw, and the boy uncovered his eyes.

"Yip! Yip! Yip!" Sparky barked loudly. *By your feet!*

Carl gazed around the Hall.

"**Yip! Yip! Yip!**" Sparky
said again. *No, down here!*

Sparky gave a little growl. He
looked at the backpack, then at
Carl, then at the backpack again.
He wagged his tail furiously.

"That way?" asked Carl, pointing to the door.

Sparky barked. *No.*

Carl smiled and sprinted out of the room.

Not out there! Sparky ran after Carl. Before he'd even left the Hall, he could smell the strong aromas of cooking. Carl had gone into the school canteen.

Sparky followed, trying to stop him. By the time Sparky got there,

Mrs Broth, the school cook, was
standing among the steaming pots
and pans with her hands on her
hips.

Carl reached up high on a shelf, tipping over a bag of flour. It poured out and floated down like snow.

"What do you think you're doing?" Mrs Broth roared at Carl, who was now opening every drawer and cupboard, searching for the crystal ball.

He picked up handfuls of cutlery and dropped them onto the worktop with a loud **clank!** that made Sparky wince.

"I'm looking for—" Carl began, spinning round to open a cupboard behind him. But he threw the door open with such force that it knocked a metal tray, which **wobbled**, then fell, spilling its entire contents into a huge mixing bowl.

Mrs Broth shrieked. Carl gasped

and put his hand to his mouth. Sparky covered his eyes with his paws.

When he dared to look he saw hundreds of bite-sized treats sinking into a glowing rainbow-coloured mixture.

"The rainbow cake!" Mrs Broth cried in horror. "It was supposed to be for the school inspectors on Monday. And those were the treats for their familiars."

"I'm so sorry," Carl said quietly. Sparky's tail drooped.

"Get out of my kitchen!" Mrs Broth demanded crossly. "Mrs Mothwick will be hearing about this."

Carl slunk out, head hanging. Sparky followed him, tail between his legs.

They'd be in even bigger trouble now.

5

"Aw, I'm never going to get this right," Carl complained the next day.

"Yip! Yip!" Sparky assured him. *You will!*

Sparky, Carl, Sophie and Sox had

snuck out of Mrs Mothwick's Magic
Academy and gone to Dead End
Valley. The hazy afternoon sunshine
was throwing strange shadows on
the ground.

Sophie looked at Carl kindly.
"Keep practising," she said. "You
and Sparky need to learn to play
fetch before Mr Carrion's next
communication class."

Sparky turned to Sox. "Tell Sophie
our code again, so she can tell Carl,"

he said. "One bark to go left. Two
barks to go right. A yip if he's going
the right way, a growl if he's not."

Sox told Sophie exactly what
Sparky had said, then Sophie
explained the code to Carl. Sparky

picked up Carl's red rubber ball and waited for Carl to close his eyes. As soon as he did, Sparky scampered off and hid the ball behind a rock near the stream.

"Open your eyes!" Sophie said.

"Woof! Woof!"

"I need to go right?" Carl asked,
and he began walking slowly
towards the stream.

"Yip!" Sparky cried. *Yes!*

Carl reached the stream, but
couldn't see the ball.

"Arrf!" Sparky barked.

"Left?" Carl asked.

"Yip!" *Carl was doing it!*

The boy looked more confident

now, and was walking quickly alongside the stream. Before Sparky had a chance to give another yip, Carl had passed the ball.

"Grrr!" Sparky growled.

Carl looked confused and scratched his head. Then he said: "Oh, I thought you meant left."

"Yip!" Sparky said. *I did mean left, but—*

"You meant right? But then I'll be in the stream and—"

"**Grrr!**" Sparky growled again. He wanted to tell Carl that the ball was just behind him, but the boy had already stepped into the stream and his shoes were getting wet.

Suddenly a strong smell made Sparky's nose sting. It was a scent he knew – half lion, half eagle. The scruff of Sparky's neck tingled as all the hairs stood on end. *Is that a . . . griffin?*

Sparky stuck his snout high in the air, trying to tell where the worrying whiff was coming from. Then something caught his eye. Trotting down the slope towards Sparky and Carl was a large dog

with soft golden fur and big brown
eyes.

"Hello there!" the hound said
cheerfully.

Sparky's tail wagged. He hadn't seen another dog since he'd left the rescue centre. They gave each other a welcoming sniff.

"My name's Rover," said the dog. "Who are you?"

"I'm Sparky!"

"I'm Carl," said Carl, shaking some water off his shoes.

Wowzers! Sparky thought. Carl can understand Rover, so he must be a—

"I'm Miss Daisy's familiar,"
Rover said. "Here she is now."

So dogs *could* be familiars!
Sparky was delighted. He wasn't
the only one after all.

Behind Rover,
a short lady was
walking down
the slope, smiling
broadly. Her black
hair was tied neatly
in a bun, and her

green eyes twinkled. She had a
large brown mole on her chin.

"Carl?" Miss Daisy said, studying
the boy's face. "Carl Mothwick?"

Carl nodded.

How does this woman know Carl?
Sparky wondered.

"Oh! How lovely to see you
again," she said, beaming.

Carl tilted his head to the side.
"Pardon me," he said. "Have we
met?"

Miss Daisy laughed. "We have, but you were very little then. Your mum and I used to be best friends. We trained together at Mr Boogletwitch's School for Young Witches and Wizards on the far side of the **Deep Dark Wood**. Of course, it's not called that any more."

"No," Carl said, grinning. "It's *Miss Spellcheck's* School for Young Witches and Wizards now. Sophie

and I go there for our regular school lessons, when we're not working with our familiars at the Magic Academy, of course."

Sophie waved shyly at Miss Daisy and said, "Hi."

"What are you all doing here?" Miss Daisy asked, frowning a little. **"The Deep Dark Wood can be a very dangerous place."**

Sparky's nose twitched. "We know," he said. "Carl and I were almost caught by a griffin once. In fact, I'm sure I can smell one round here—"

"A griffin?" Rover chortled. "If there was a griffin, I'd be able to smell it, but I can't smell a thing!"

Sparky glanced around. The scent was still there, but he couldn't see any sign of a griffin. Sparky shivered a little but felt more at ease when Carl ruffled his ears.

"We came here to practise playing fetch," Carl told Miss Daisy. "Sparky and I can't talk to each other and there's a school inspection on Monday.

Mum said if the Council thinks we're
training an un-magic puppy, the
school might be closed down."

"Dearie me!" Miss Daisy gasped.
"Mrs Mothwick's Magic Academy
closed down? That would be terrible."

"I know," Carl sighed, his
shoulders slumping.

"Do you young wizards still use
crystal balls to play fetch with?" Miss
Daisy asked.

Carl nodded.

"Hmm," Miss Daisy said, looking thoughtful. "Well then, there is one thing you could try, just to pass the school inspection."

Sparky's ears pricked up.

"What's that?" Carl asked.

"Well, if you had another crystal ball, and you kept it with you, you could just pretend to find the one Sparky has hidden. When no one is looking, simply bring the second ball out of your coat pocket!"

"I'm not sure . . ." Carl said, frowning.

Sparky wasn't sure either. At least with their code they had found a way of communicating without magic. Miss Daisy's idea sounded like plain cheating.

"You'd be in big trouble if you got caught," Sophie said. Sox's ears flattened.

Rover raised one furry eyebrow. "You wouldn't want your school to be shut down though, would you, Carl?" he asked.

Sparky's ears drooped. That would be awful – worse than cheating.

Miss Daisy clapped her hands

happily. "I'm sure it'll work, and I have a spare crystal ball you can borrow."

Carl looked worried for a moment, but then made up his mind. "OK. Thank you."

Sparky watched Miss Daisy as she walked up the slope towards the cave. She returned quickly, holding a crystal ball. A tiny wisp of smoke curled out from it, but Miss

Daisy batted it away into the air
with her hand.

"Here," she said, holding the ball
out for Carl. "Take good care of it."

Carl took it and looked at it
closely.

"Goodness, we'd better be off,
Rover!" Miss Daisy said shrilly.
"The sun will be going down soon,
so you children had better get
back, too."

Rover and Miss Daisy hurried up

the slope and out of sight.

"I don't suppose you need to practise now that you're cheating," Sophie said to Carl, not looking at him, "but Sox and I still should."

Sophie gave Sox her sparkly purple hair clip. The kitten bounced off and hid it near the stream, behind a spiky yellow plant.

When Sox came back, she tried to communicate with Sophie. "Mew! Prr-eam! Miaow! Prr-ant!"

Sophie looked blankly at
Sox. "What?" she said. "I can't
understand you."

That's strange, Sparky
thought. *Sox is usually really good at
talking to Sophie.* He gave his friend
a reassuring grin.

Sox tried again. "Mew! Prr-eam!
Miaow! Prr-ant!"

"Sorry, Sox. I'm just hearing
miaows and purrs." Sophie sighed.
"Come on, let's all go back before
someone realizes we're missing."

Sox looked upset, so Sparky
gave her a nuzzle. "Maybe you're

just tired," he suggested.

Frustrated, they all headed off up
the path towards the school.

Before Sparky followed them,
he glanced back and, for a brief
moment, he saw a

long dark shadow

looming on the ground.
Sparky gasped and dashed after
Carl. The puppy really hoped it was

just his imagination, but whatever
had made that shadow looked like
it had a very large beak.

6

Finley squealed, leaping through a hoop and landing with a **roly-poly.**
Mr Noble was taking PE class and the Courtyard was set out like an obstacle course.

As well as hoops, there were ramps, tunnels and miniature walls.

"You have ten minutes to complete the course," Mr Noble announced. "Begin!"

Sparky dashed towards a tunnel and sped through it.

"Good boy!" Carl said. "Now, up!"

Running as fast as he could and with his fluffy ears flip-flapping, Sparky leaped high into the air,

right over the first wall. He was
about to jump through a hoop,
when Mr Noble stepped in front of
him.

Sparky banged his nose on Mr
Noble's shins and sneezed.

"Er, Carl," Mr Noble said. "This
is a magical obstacle course. Sparky
should be using magic to run
through the walls, not jumping over
them . . ."

Sparky whined. Up ahead, Gill

the goldfish was floating in his bowl
through a series of hoops. Each one
whizzed round like a Catherine
wheel as he passed through it. Trixie
pounced off a ramp, and instead of
landing back on the ground,

102

she floated in mid-air.

"Wheee!" she cried, twirling gracefully.

"Look at Trixie, everyone!" Amelia said proudly. "I bet none of your familiars can do that."

Trixie landed and gave a little bow, then she sauntered over to Sparky. "Still not managing any magic, un-magic puppy? You know it's only a matter of time, don't you? Before someone realizes . . . or someone tells."

Sparky didn't reply. It was better to ignore Trixie when she was being mean. He turned his back and ambled over to Sox and Sophie. They both looked very worried.

"I don't know what's happened," Sox said. "I can't get through the wall, and Sophie still can't understand what I'm saying. *My magic has gone!*"

"Don't worry," Sparky soothed. "I'm sure the magic will come back."

Bang! Bang! Bang!

Three loud knocks echoed through the Courtyard. Mr Noble looked up towards the stone

serpents curled around the school's spires. Sparky jumped when one of the serpents stretched out, peering over the school walls to see who was waiting beyond the drawbridge. It nodded slowly.

Mr Noble strode to the
drawbridge and began to lower
it, just as Mrs Mothwick hurried
out of the school, looking hot and
bothered. Her eyes were wide and
she was biting her bottom lip.

The heavy drawbridge clunked
down to the ground. Three smartly
dressed people and their familiars
were standing at the entrance to
the school.

There was a large man with a

round tummy and scruffy brown
hair, who had a tawny owl on his
shoulder.

Next to him stood a stocky lady
with hazel eyes and a wide smile.
A warty toad was peeping out of
her bag.

Behind the lady was a short
man. His head was completely bald
but he had bushy black eyebrows
and a grey moustache. In his arms
was a tubby black cat with long
silver whiskers.

"What a pleasant surprise!"
Mrs Mothwick said, holding

out a slightly shaky hand. "Mr Broomstickler! Miss Frownbaum! Mr Balding! We thought the inspection was on Monday."

The school inspectors! Sparky realized. *They're three days early!*

Mr Carrion swooped into the Courtyard while Mr Noble pulled up the drawbridge. "Mr Tawny," Mr Carrion said warmly to the ancient owl. "You look well."

Mr Tawny flew down from

Mr Broomstickler's shoulder, and tapped his brown tummy with his wings. "I've been eating well!" he chortled.

"Miss Lily and Mrs Whiskerson," Mr Carrion continued. "Welcome to Mrs Mothwick's Magic Academy."

Mrs Mothwick and Mr Carrion led the inspectors and their

familiars across the Courtyard.

"You're all training hard, I
hope," Mr Tawny said loudly as he
passed the young animals. When
he saw Sparky, his round eyes grew
even rounder. He leaned towards Mr
Carrion and said hoarsely, "Good
grief, a few things have
changed since our day."

Sparky cowered
a little.

"You old grumps!"

Miss Lily croaked at them. "Just because there wasn't a magic dog in our day doesn't mean there can't be one now."

Sparky wagged his tail nervously. *It's strange they haven't heard of Rover*, he thought.

"You're welcome to wander as you please," Mrs Mothwick blustered. "We've nothing to hide here!"

"Is that young Carl?" Mr Balding asked, pointing. "He's grown!

Perhaps he and his familiar could show us round?"

All the trainees in Carl's class gasped, then tried to look like they hadn't.

Mrs Mothwick cleared her throat loudly. "Er, yes, of course! Come along, Carl."

Carl shuffled forward and shook Mr Balding's hand. Sparky trotted beside him, with his head hanging close to the floor. He glanced

nervously at Mrs Whiskerson.

What if they realize? he thought,
remembering Trixie's unkind words.

"Maybe Amelia and Trixie could
help, too?" Mrs Mothwick suggested.
"There's so much to see."

Trixie pranced towards the
inspectors with her tail in the air.

Yes please, Sparky thought.
*No one will pay any attention to me
when Trixie's showing off.*

"Excellent idea," Mr Balding said.

"You can take the others around the main school while Carl and Sparky show me the Magic Lab."

Mr Broomstickler, Mr Tawny, Miss Frownbaum and Miss Lily followed Amelia inside.

"I'm one of seventeen generations of familiars," Trixie told Mr Tawny as they followed.

Carl glanced at Mr Balding, then said, "Please follow us."

Sparky scampered across the

Courtyard to a heavy wooden
door carved with the words: MAGIC
LABORATORY – CAUTION! Carl pushed
the door open.

Inside, six huge black cauldrons
were boiling furiously, each giving
off different-coloured steam. Sparky
sniffed the air. It was full of all sorts of
smells: pickles, coal, snails, mulberries,
mistletoe and even dove feathers.

"Lots of potions cooking here,"
Mr Balding said cheerfully, peering
into a cauldron full of bubbling
red slime. When each bubble

pOpped, a musical note rang out. Together the popping bubbles made a twinkly tune. Mrs Whiskerson jumped onto a shelf to get a better view and Sparky scrambled onto a stool, then a counter.

"Safety is our top priority," Carl said proudly.

Well done, Carl! Sparky thought

to himself, wagging his tail. He had heard Mrs Mothwick say those exact words a hundred times before.

"Oh!" Mrs Whiskerson said suddenly. "Sparky, mind the—"

Too late! Sparky's wagging tail knocked a tall jar of bright pink magical powder off the counter, and it toppled

towards the steaming cauldron.

Carl gasped. Sparky cowered, waiting for a big **bang!**

But the jar stopped in mid-air. For a second, Sparky could see a blue shimmering dome over the cauldron. The jar slowly slid down the dome, and Mr Balding caught it with his right hand.

"How clever!" Mr Balding cried. "An invisible force-field to prevent accidents. Thank you, Sparky, for that excellent demonstration."

Sparky tried not to look surprised
when he saw it – he had no idea the
force-field was there. He glanced at
Carl, who silently mouthed, "Phew!"
He obviously had no idea it was there
either.

Behind Carl, Mrs Whiskerson
was smiling. "Sparky, did I hear you
used to live at Green Meadow Rescue
Centre?" she asked.

Sparky's ears immediately drooped.
"Yes," the puppy replied quietly.

He didn't want to talk about the rescue centre. Most of the animals at the school had come from generations of familiars – unlike him and Sox.

"I remember the centre well," Mrs Whiskerson continued.

Sparky looked at her in astonishment.

"Yes, Sparky! I was adopted from there, too. **And if I became an accomplished familiar,**

**then there's no reason
why you can't either."**

Sparky's tail wagged and he gave
a happy sigh.

"Everyone at this school should
be judged by their actions," she said.
"Not by where they were brought
up, or how many generations of
familiars they come from."

She purred kindly at Sparky, and
he wagged his tail.

Mr Balding placed his clipboard

on the counter, and took a red pen
from his top pocket. "Now, where
is it," Mr Balding muttered as he
searched for the right section on his
form. Sparky watched nervously,
wondering what Mr Balding was
going to write.

Mr Balding
smiled as he put
a large red tick in
the box next to the
words "Magic Lab".

MAGIC LAB ✓

comments:
Excellent force-
field demonstration

Yes! Sparky thought. *The school will pass the inspection. It's going to be all right!*

MRS MOTHWICK'S MAGIC ACADEMY

7

"Oh, there you are," Mrs Mothwick said nervously when she saw Sparky and Carl leading Mr Balding and Mrs Whiskerson out into the Courtyard. "I hope everything was to your satisfaction?"

"Oh, yes!" Mr Balding replied. "The Magic Lab was superb, and Sparky's safety demonstration was very impressive."

Mrs Mothwick gave Sparky a questioning look, so he glanced away.

Mr Broomstickler waved his clipboard in the air. The paper was covered in red ticks. "Everything seems to be in order, Mrs Mothwick," he said, smiling.

"The Magic Academy has passed with flying colours."

Sparky gave a happy yip! Carl grinned and bent down to ruffle his puppy's ears.

"I'm so pleased," Mrs Mothwick said, with a long sigh of relief. Then she lowered her voice. "But would you mind me asking why you came to visit us three days early?"

Mr Broomstickler leaned towards

Mrs Mothwick. Sparky pricked his ears so he could hear the man's hushed tones.

"Between you and me," Mr Broomstickler said quietly, "we received an anonymous tip. Someone contacted the

Council to say there was a non-magic animal being trained at your school."

Mrs Mothwick looked shocked. Sparky lowered his head and stared at the ground, hoping no one would look at him.

Trixie! he thought. *It must have been Trixie and Amelia. They've always been cross about me being here.*

Yet something didn't seem quite right. Trixie was mean, but would

she really risk their school being closed, just to get rid of Sparky?

Mr Broomstickler roared with laughter and patted Mrs Mothwick hard on the back. "We had to check, but what nonsense! As if you would ever train an un-magic animal!"

"Of course not," Mrs Mothwick spluttered. "Now, perhaps you would all like a quick cup of tea before you leave?"

Miss Frownbaum put down her

bag and glanced at a watch on her chubby wrist. "Oh, there's no need for us to rush off just yet," she said cheerfully. "In fact, we'd love to see your familiars in action."

"Er, yes . . ." Mrs Mothwick replied, looking worried again.

Mr Carrion cleared his throat and stepped in front of her. "Trixie and Amelia, Finley and Joshua," he called. "Why don't you demonstrate 'fetch' for our inspectors? Sophie, go

and get the crystal balls."

The trainees and their familiars stepped forward, while Sophie hurried indoors. She returned quickly with the heavy wicker basket.

"What about Carl and Sparky?" Mr Balding asked.

No! Sparky thought. *Please don't ask us!* Carl started chewing nervously on his fingernails.

"I very much enjoyed the tour they gave me," Mr Balding said

eagerly. "I'd love to see them
working together."

"Well . . ." said Mrs Mothwick.

Say no, say no! Sparky willed her.
He glanced up at Carl, who had his
fingers crossed.

Mrs Mothwick
paused. She took
a hanky from
her sleeve,
dabbed her
sweaty forehead

with it, then said, "Yes, all right."

Sparky's heart sank.

While Sophie began handing out
the crystal balls, Carl stooped down.

"Let's try our code again," he said
to Sparky. "One bark for left, two
barks for right. A yip if I'm going
the right way, a growl if I'm not.
Yes?"

"Yip!" Sparky replied. Sox was
sitting with the other familiars,
watching. She gave Sparky an
encouraging smile.

Mr Carrion took his wand out
from under his wings. He tapped
the crystal balls in turn, until each

one had an image of its trainee and familiar inside the glass.

"I'm really looking forward to watching the puppy," Miss Frownbaum said to Miss Lily. "I've never even heard of a canine familiar before!"

Miss Lily gave a happy

Ribbet!

and leaped onto Miss

Frownbaum's shoulder for a better view. Sparky gulped hard. He wanted to mention Rover, but now wasn't the time to compare himself to other familiars, even dog ones.

"Familiars," Mr Carrion squawked loudly. "Hide your crystal balls somewhere inside the school. Begin!"

The witches and wizards covered their eyes. Finley immediately picked up his crystal ball in his

teeth and scurried off. Trixie gave
a little yawn, licked her paw a few
times, and then expertly rolled her
ball towards the school building.

*I need to make it really easy for Carl
to find*, Sparky thought to himself.
He picked up the ball in his mouth
and hid it right behind the open
door of the school.

Sparky scampered back to Carl,
and quietly growled when Trixie
shoved past him.

"Yip!" Sparky said. Carl opened his eyes.

"Woof!" Sparky barked once.

"Left," Carl said under his breath. He turned to his left and began walking towards the entrance to the school. Sparky waited until Carl had stepped right inside, then he barked again.

"Woof! Woof!"

Carl looked at him. "Right," he said.

Sparky yipped to tell Carl he was doing well, and the boy took two steps to his right.

"Woof! Woof!" Sparky barked. *If Carl turns right again now, he'll see the ball!*

Carl turned right again. Now he was behind the open door.

Sparky gave a "Yip!"

Carl looked at Sparky and raised his hands in the air. "Where now, boy?" he asked.

Right there! he thought. Then Sparky looked at the floor and gasped in surprise.

The crystal ball had gone!

"Grrrr," Sparky growled. He
sniffed at the floor hard.

Carl was scratching his head.
"I did it wrong again, didn't I?"
the boy asked glumly.

Sparky yipped and growled and
barked. He didn't know how to tell
Carl. *You didn't do it wrong! The ball
was here! This is where I left it!*

Amelia stepped out into the
courtyard, holding a crystal ball.
"Found it! Easy peasy."

"I'm so sorry, Sparky," Carl said, peeping round the door towards the inspectors. "I really didn't want to cheat, but if we don't take a crystal ball back, they might close down the school."

Sparky whined quietly.

"Miss Daisy's ball is in my room. Wait here, and don't let the inspectors see you!"

Carl ran off, skidding round a corner. He was back within a

minute, holding Miss Daisy's
crystal ball.

"Ready?" Carl asked.

"Yip!" Sparky replied, and he
followed Carl into the Courtyard,
where Amelia was talking to Mr
Broomstickler.

"We are usually the first ones
back," she told him, flicking her
ponytail. "Trixie and I are naturals
at communicating. We have such
a strong bond. Playing fetch is

very simple for us."

Mrs Mothwick spun round as Carl cleared his throat. She looked both surprised and delighted to see him returning with a crystal ball in his hand. Mr Carrion's beak opened in shock.

"Found it," Carl said quietly, flashing an uneasy smile at his mum.

Amelia stopped talking to Mr Broomstickler and gasped when she saw Carl and Sparky. **"They've cheated!"** the girl said sharply. "They've definitely cheated. That's not their ball!"

Sparky's tail stopped wagging. *Oh no!* he thought. *We're in really, really big trouble this time.*

8

"Cheated?" Mrs Mothwick boomed, glaring at Carl. Sparky cowered behind Carl's legs and whimpered.

"Hang on a minute," Sophie interrupted. She picked up Sox and walked over to Amelia. "How

do you know Carl and Sparky
cheated?"

Mrs Mothwick turned to Amelia
and looked at the girl suspiciously.

"That's a good point, Sophie,"
Mrs Mothwick said thoughtfully.
She took three brisk steps towards
Amelia, scooped the crystal ball
out of the girl's hands, and peered
into it.

"This is Carl and Sparky's ball!"
Mrs Mothwick gasped, holding it up

so everyone could see the picture of Carl and Sparky inside.

Sparky growled loudly. *Trixie and Amelia took our ball!*

"How *terrible*," Miss Frownbaum tutted.

"What do you have to say for yourself, young lady?" Mrs Mothwick asked, wagging her finger in Amelia's direction.

Amelia didn't reply. Her cheeks
went pink and she stared at the
ground.

Trixie's ears flattened. "We wanted to be the first ones back," she whined. "We wanted to be the best."

A few of the other witches were nudging each other and whispering.

"That's no excuse for cheating," said Miss Lily.

"Or taking Carl and Sparky's ball," added Mrs Whiskerson.

"Silence, witches!" Mr Carrion

screeched. Next to him, Mr Tawny
looked sternly at the young
animals, and ruffled his feathers.

"I'll deal with you two later," Mrs
Mothwick said to Amelia quietly.
Then she walked back to Carl and
lifted his chin with a bony finger.

"If Amelia and Trixie have *your* ball," she said, "then whose ball do you have?"

Carl didn't look at his mum, but he held up Miss Daisy's crystal ball for her to see. As he did so, two tiny

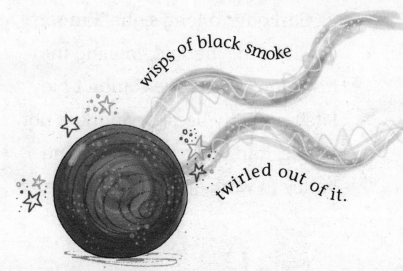

wisps of black smoke twirled out of it.

Mrs Mothwick gasped. "Tell me where you got this!"

Sparky trembled. "I'm really sorry," he said.

"Speak up!" Mrs Mothwick ordered.

Carl gave a long sigh. "I'm sorry we cheated," he said, looking into his mum's eyes. "We couldn't play fetch properly because Sparky's not magic, and we went to Dead End Valley to work out a special code.

That didn't work, but we met a really nice witch called Miss Daisy – your school friend – and she said we could borrow her crystal ball so we could just pretend we had found our ball, and . . ."

Carl paused. Sparky whined. Mrs Mothwick's eyes were wide.

"Not magic?" Mr Balding said under his breath.

The inspectors began murmuring among themselves.

Miss Lily gave a loud, surprised **Ribbet!**

"I really didn't want Sparky to be sent away," Carl added quietly. "He's my best friend." Sparky nuzzled Carl's ankles.

"This witch, Miss Daisy," Mrs Mothwick said, looking confused. "What did she look like?"

Carl scratched his head. "She had black hair, in a bun. Green

eyes. She was
quite short.
Oh! And she
had a big
brown mole,
right here."
Carl pointed to
the tip of his chin.

Mrs Mothwick's mouth dropped
open and she looked at Mr Carrion.

"Oh dear, oh dear," the old
vulture muttered, shaking his head.

"What is it?" Carl asked.

"That wasn't Miss Daisy," Mrs Mothwick replied. **"It was the evil Mrs Cackleback! I *knew* she was close by!"**

"But she said she was your friend!" Carl exclaimed.

"We used to be friends . . . a long time ago," Mrs Mothwick explained quietly. "She was a talented young witch." She looked sad. "Then

she began practising wicked ways
and—"

Carl was looking surprised now.

"Well," Mrs Mothwick continued,
"now she is a very dangerous
woman."

Sparky was confused. "It can't
have been Mrs Cackleback," he
said. "You told us her familiar was
a griffin. But the lady we met had a
dog. His name was Rover."

"Ha! A *canine* familiar?" Mr

Carrion snorted unkindly. "Mrs Cackleback is a powerful witch. It would have been easy for her to disguise her griffin by making him look like a dog. She must have used the Shift Shape Spell."

Sparky's ears drooped. Suddenly it all made sense. *That's why I could smell a griffin,* he thought to himself. *I should have trusted my nose!*

"I think we have heard enough!" Mr Broomstickler bellowed. Miss

Frownbaum was standing behind
him looking horrified. Mr Balding
was frantically writing something
on his clipboard.

Mrs Mothwick turned to face the inspectors. She opened her mouth to speak, but no words came out.

"Mrs Mothwick," Mr Broom-stickler said, peering down his nose at her, "as the head of this school it is your job to protect all these young students. Yet Mrs Cackleback managed to befriend your own son! You have put the trainees in grave danger."

Carl glanced at the crystal ball

in his hands. *Another wisp of black smoke twirled off it*

and floated past his mum.

Mr Tawny flapped his wings, flew a neat circle in the air, and landed on Mr Broomstickler's shoulder. "What is more," the owl said to Mrs Mothwick, "it is now clear that you have been training an un-magic animal. This is very serious indeed."

Mr Broomstickler ripped the

paper with all the ticks off his clipboard. He screwed it up into a ball, and threw it on the ground.

"We shall be reporting back to the GRAND COUNCIL OF WIZARDRY AND WITCHINESS this afternoon," he said sharply. "You will hear by the end of the week whether your academy will be allowed to remain open."

Trixie gasped and Amelia brought her hand to her mouth. Sparky realized that they had no

idea what their cheating would do.

"In the meantime," Mrs Frownbaum said, "send that puppy back to wherever he came from."

"*No! Please don't send me away!*" Sparky whined loudly.

Carl grabbed Mrs Mothwick's hand. "Please, Mum!"

"Of course the dog can't stay!" Mr Tawny hooted. "He has no magic in him at all. He can't even communicate with his wizard—"

Suddenly a horrible smell stung Sparky's nose and made him shiver. Half lion, half eagle! It was a stench that Sparky would never forget. *A griffin!*

High above, a strong gust of

wind blew a dark cloud across the sky, blocking out the sun. There was a **crash!** that sounded like thunder. Black smoke billowed above the Courtyard. Sparky flinched as he heard an ear-splitting screech and the ***Whoosh! Whoosh! Whoosh!*** of two huge wings beating.

Sparky looked up – and yipped with fright!

Out from the black cloud
emerged Mrs Cackleback, riding
a huge and terrifying griffin. Her
black hair was not tied neatly in
a bun now; it was long, wild and
wiry. Her green eyes were staring
and wide. On her chin was a huge
brown mole.

The evil witch cackled as she
zoomed through the air, right over
the high wall of the school and
then down . . .

9

"Nee-hee-hee-hee!" Mrs Cackleback's hideous laugh echoed around the Courtyard as she shot towards the ground.

All the witches were staring at her in terror. Familiars were

scrambling to hide in their
witch's pockets.

"You stupid
do-gooders!"
Mrs Cackleback
shrieked. "How
easy it was to fool

a Mothwick! Now I'm going to use all your own powers against you!"

"Everyone!" Mrs Mothwick shouted. "Get inside, now!"

The young witches and wizards began running towards the school,

but the doors slammed shut, one by one. Everyone started scrambling in different directions, unsure of which way to go.

The griffin dipped its beak and twirled into a steep nose-dive. Sparky yipped and barked and growled. *Oh no! The griffin's heading straight for Carl!*

The boy was running towards the Magic Lab – but he wasn't running fast enough.

The griffin's right behind Carl! It's going to get him!

"Woof! Carrf! Carrlf!" Sparky shouted as loudly as he could. **"CARL! DUCK!"**

Carl's eyes widened and he ducked just as the griffin swooped past him. Mrs Cackleback snatched at the crystal ball in the boy's hands but she couldn't reach it.

She wants the ball! Sparky thought.

The griffin soared up into the air and flew in a huge circle before starting to swoop down again.

Mrs Mothwick and the inspectors pulled their wands from their sleeves, as Mrs Mothwick bellowed:

"Razzle-be-dazzle! Ickra-bazzoo!

Be gone, evil witch, and your wicked ways too!"

Mrs Mothwick and the inspectors

all flicked their wands sharply towards Mrs Cackleback – but nothing happened. They tried again. Their wands weren't working!

"What's happening?" Mrs Mothwick cried. "Where's the magic?"

"Nee-hee-hee-hee!"

Mrs Cackleback shrieked. "I've captured it, you silly woman. And I used your precious son and his stupid, bouncy mongrel puppy to do it!"

Sparky shook with fear.

The grown-ups had lost their magic, just like Sophie and Sox had

done after Mrs Cackleback gave
Carl the crystal ball.

That's it! Sparky thought. *That's
why she wants the ball!* His mind was
racing. Those black wisps of smoke
meant the magic of wicked ways.
The smoke had twirled around the
Courtyard, around Mrs Mothwick
and all the inspectors. The crystal
ball had captured all the magic!
**Whoosh! Whoosh!
Whoosh!** The griffin was diving

back down towards the ground,
heading straight for Carl again.

"Woof! Carrf! Carrlf!" Sparky
shouted. **"Carl! Throw the
ball. Smash it!"**

Carl briefly looked at the crystal
ball in his hand, then turned and
threw it as hard as he could against
the wall of the school.

There was a loud *bang!*

And then a **flash!** As the ball
smashed, five glittering golden

ribbons of light swirled out and
whizzed across the Courtyard
towards Sophie, Mrs Mothwick
and the inspectors. The ribbons

disappeared into the witches' and
wizards' chests, each one creating
a **_puff!_** of golden glitter.

"Now!" Mrs Mothwick
yelled, waving her wand at Mrs
Cackleback.

The inspectors flicked their
wands too. This time, blinding
flashes shot towards the evil witch.

"Nooo!" Mrs Cackleback
screeched. The griffin swooped high
into the air, twisting left and right

to avoid the torrent of magical
sparks.

"I'll be back!" Mrs Cackleback's
piercing voice echoed as they flew
away over the school wall. "I'll
make you all sorry for this!"

Sparky watched, panting, as the griffin disappeared into the distance. High in the sky, a dark cloud shifted and sunlight streamed down into the Courtyard again. The young trainees and their familiars gathered around Sparky.

"Well done, Sparky," Finley the Ferret squeaked.

"Three cheers for Sparky!" cried Sox. "He saved the day!"

"Hip hip – hooray!

Hip hip – hooray!
Hip hip – hooray!"

But Sparky was just worried
about Carl – his face had gone
ghostly white. Sparky pawed the
boy's shoe.

"Good dog," Carl said,
bending down.
Sparky leaped into
his arms and
licked him all
over his face.

"Yip! Yip! Yip!" Sparky said.
Phew! You're OK!

Sox jumped
up on her hind
paws. "That was
amazing!" she
purred happily.

"I know!"
Sparky replied.
"Mrs Mothwick's magic is really
powerful—"

"Not Mrs Mothwick, silly!" Sox

said, smiling. "You! Don't you realize what you just did?"

Sparky wasn't sure what Sox meant.

Sox playfully rolled her eyes at him. "Sparky, you spoke to Carl! In words!" she said. "You told Carl to duck, and you told him to smash the ball, and he understood you!"

Sparky gasped. *I did! I spoke to Carl!* **"Wowzers!"**

"Well, well," Miss Lily said,

giving Mr Tawny a sideways look. "Maybe a dog can be trained to be a familiar after all."

"Nonsense," Mr Tawny replied, puffing out the feathers on his chest. "There must be some mistake."

"There was no mistake, Mr Tawny," Mrs Whiskerson said softly. "Sparky is learning to be a familiar."

Mr Carrion grumbled something

under his breath, but Sparky wagged
his tail hard, making Carl giggle.

Mr Broomstickler cleared
his throat. "I agree with Mrs
Whiskerson," he said. "And, Mrs
Mothwick, you have shown you are
able to protect the young trainees at
your excellent school. We will present
our findings to the Grand Council."

Mrs Mothwick gave the inspectors
a broad smile. "Thank you," she
said, "and thank goodness everyone

is safe. Thank you most of all, Sparky. Once again, you saved my son."

Sparky's tail wagged frantically. He felt very proud of himself.

Mr Carrion showed the inspectors and their familiars out across the drawbridge, then hopped over to Mrs Mothwick.

Carl's mum brushed down her long black dress and dabbed at her forehead with her hanky. Then she turned to the witches, wizards and familiars.

"As I said before," Mrs Mothwick said sternly, "we do not stand for cheating in this school." Her eyes

flicked between Carl and Amelia.
"We will discuss fair punishments
tomorrow, agreed?"

Carl mumbled, "Yes, Mum."

Amelia just nodded.

"Good!" Mrs Mothwick smiled.
"Now, after all that excitement, I
think we need some refreshments.
Everyone go to the Dining Hall.
Mrs Broth has prepared sandwiches
and crumpets for the witches and
wizards, and there is something

extra special for the familiars."

"Yum, what are we having?" Finley asked, licking his lips.

"It's a colourful rainbow cake," Mrs Mothwick replied. "Not just any cake though: it's filled with special treats for familiars!"

She gave Carl and Sparky a little wink.

Sox and Finley bounded inside
and the other familiars began
trotting in behind them.

Sparky nuzzled Carl's collar.
"Yip! Yip! Arrfan! Stay!" he said. *I'm
so happy I can stay!*

"Stay?" Carl said. "Er . . ."

Carl didn't understand, so Sparky
gave him a big wet lick on the nose.

"Hey, stop!" Carl laughed. Then
he ruffled Sparky's ears and said,
"I love you too."

"Yip!" It didn't matter to Sparky that he couldn't always use words. He and Carl had their own way of communicating, and it worked just fine.

Trixie and Amelia were the last ones to go back into the school.

"He's still un-magic," Trixie whispered as she walked past. "He'll never be good enough. He's bound to bring down the good name of the school."

Sparky watched Trixie disappear through the arched wooden doors, his mind whirring. Was it Trixie and Amelia who had called the inspectors? Would Trixie risk the school being closed just to get rid of him?

I'll prove myself to Trixie, he thought happily. **I'm going to prove that anyone can learn to be magic – even a bouncy mongrel puppy like me!**

Read on for some magical games and activities!

Mr Carrion's Cunning Quiz

1) What did Amelia's great-great-grandmother invent?

2) What dangerous things can you find in the **Deep Dark Wood**?

3) What is a Shift Root used for?

4) What does a Shift Root smell like?

5) What sort of animal does Mrs Cackleback turn her familiar into?

6) What familiars do the inspectors have?

7) Where did Mrs Whiskerson use to live?

8) Who steals Carl and Sparky's crystal ball?

Turn to the back of the book to see the answers!

Communication Code breaker

Help Sparky and Carl communicate! Using the code below, can you work out what Sparky is saying?

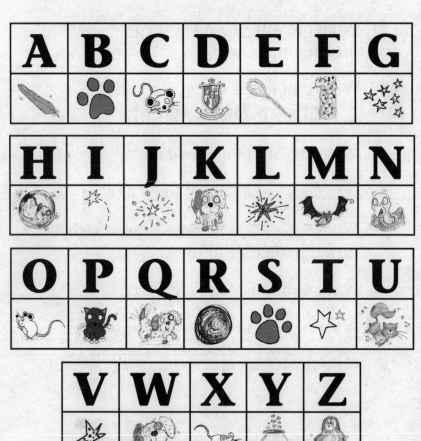

1)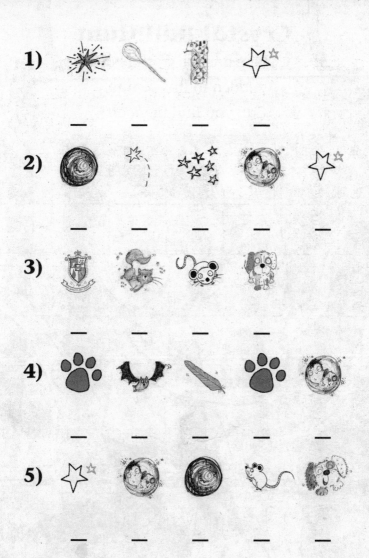

— — — —

2)

— — — — —

3)

— — — —

4)

— — — — —

5)

— — — — —

Turn to the back of the book to see the answers!

Crystal Ball Hunt

There are five crystal balls
hidden in this picture.
Can you find them all?

Turn to the back of the book to see the answers!

Witchy Wordsearch

Ten words are hidden in the
wordsearch. Can you find them all?

Homework

Rainbow

Puppy

Toad

Magical

Cat

Owl

Council

Trick

Cauldron

R	X	K	R	O	W	E	M	O	H
C	A	U	L	D	R	O	N	B	J
S	E	I	V	R	O	W	M	S	F
N	P	L	N	E	I	L	Q	A	D
E	Q	F	P	B	A	T	Y	Z	X
C	X	Y	A	U	O	S	D	L	P
T	P	I	P	L	X	W	Y	Q	E
R	U	T	L	I	C	N	U	O	C
I	P	U	P	P	Y	L	D	B	A
C	A	S	N	X	I	D	A	O	T
K	U	N	L	A	C	I	G	A	M

Turn to the back of the book to see the answers!

207

Mrs Mothwick's Maze

Find the Shift Root in the middle of the maze,
but avoid the grabby trees and gulp pits!

start

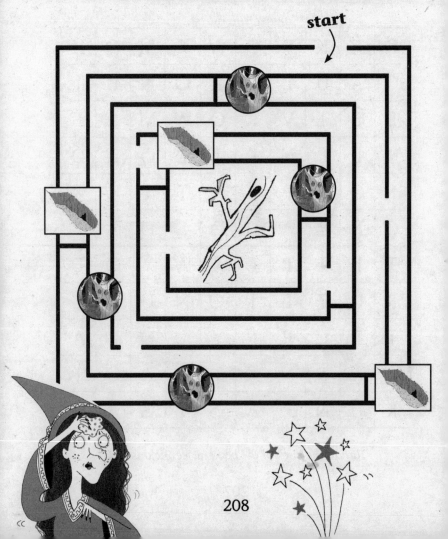

Mrs Broth's Rainbow Cake

Make sure to ask an adult to help
you make this delicious rainbow cake!

Serves twelve hungry witches, wizards or humans

Ingredients

- 350g soft butter
- 350g caster sugar
- 6 large eggs
- 350g self-raising flour
- 1 tablespoon vanilla extract
- Up to 40ml semi-skimmed milk
- Edible food colouring – red, orange, yellow, green, blue and purple

Frosting Ingredients

- 100g soft butter
- 250g cream cheese (at room temperature)
- 600g sifted icing sugar

Utensils

- 6 bowls
- A heat-proof bowl
- A wooden spoon, and six regular spoons
- A tablespoon
- 6 disposable cake cases or regular cake tins
- A skewer or a knife
- A whisk or a fork
- A sieve

Making the cake

- Preheat your oven to gas mark 4 or 170°C.
- Mix the butter and sugar in a bowl until it has combined.
- Add the eggs one at a time, followed by the flour and the vanilla extract. Mix everything well with a wooden spoon.
- If your mixture is a little too thick, add up to 40ml of semi-skimmed milk. Add a tablespoon at a time and stop when you get to a consistency that you like.
- Evenly divide your cake mix into six bowls, one for each colour. Drizzle a few drops of food colouring into each one, and stir well, using a clean spoon for each bowl.
- Pour the cake mix into disposable cake cases or just regular cake tins.

- Ask an adult to pop them into the oven for you. Be careful as the oven will be very hot!
- The cakes should take about 20 minutes to bake. Ask an adult to test if they're done by poking a skewer or a knife into each cake – if the skewer comes out clean, they're ready.
- When your cakes are cool you can start frosting them or you can wrap them in cling film and pop them into the fridge for a day. This will make the cake much easier to decorate.

Making the frosting

- Melt the butter in a heat-proof bowl in the microwave for 20–30 seconds, until it's nearly melted. Thoroughly whisk the butter until no lumps remain.
- Whisk in your cream cheese until no lumps remain.
- Sieve the icing sugar into the cream-cheese mixture, 150g at a time. Stir gently with a wooden spoon every time you add more icing sugar.
- Pop the frosting into the fridge to chill.

Assembling the rainbow cake

- Place the purple cake onto a plate or a cake stand.
- Frost the top of the purple cake with a thin layer of frosting.
- Place the blue cake on top of the purple. Spread some frosting on top of the blue.
- Place the green cake on top of the blue.
- Put the cake into the fridge for thirty minutes to chill.
- Spread some frosting on the green cake and then put the yellow cake on top.
- Spread some frosting on the yellow cake and then place the orange cake on top.

And there you have it!
One magical rainbow cake!

Answers

Mr Carrion's Cunning Quiz:

1) A thousand potions
2) Grabby trees and gulp pits
3) The Shift Shape Spell
4) Modelling clay
5) A dog
6) An owl, a toad and a cat
7) Green Meadow Rescue Centre
8) Amelia and Trixie

Communication Code Breaker:

1) Left
2) Right
3) Duck
4) Smash
5) Throw

Crystal Ball Hunt

Witchy Wordsearch

R	X	K	R	O	W	E	M	O	H
C	A	U	L	D	R	O	N	B	J
S	E	I	V	R	O	W	U	S	F
N	P	L	N	E	I	L	Q	A	D
E	Q	F	P	B	A	T	Y	Z	X
C	X	Y	A	U	O	S	D	L	P
T	P	I	P	L	X	W	Y	Q	E
R	U	T	L	I	C	N	U	O	C
I	P	U	P	P	Y	L	D	B	A
C	A	S	N	X	I	D	A	O	T
K	U	N	L	A	C	I	G	A	M

Mrs Mothwick's Maze:

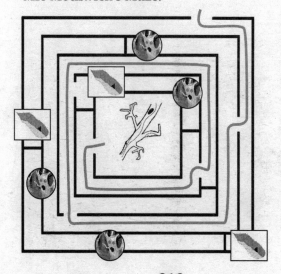

213

Coming Soon!

Sparky's School Trip

Don't miss Sparky's next adventure!